To Peter, with love ~
JB
To Nina, with love ~
RB

First published in 2011 by Scholastic Children's Books
This edition published in 2012
Euston House, 24 Eversholt Street
London NW1 1DB
a division of Scholastic Ltd
www.scholastic.com
London ~ New York ~ Toronto ~ Sydney ~ Auckland
Mexico City ~ New Delhi ~ Hong Kong

Text copyright © 2011 Janet Bingham
Illustrations copyright © 2011 Rosalind Beardshaw

ISBN 978 1 435 1 4481 1

1 3 5 7 9 10 8 6 4 2

The moral rights of Janet Bingham and Rosalind Beardshaw have been asserted.

Papers used by Scholastic Children's Books are made from
wood grown in sustainable forests.

Little Deer Lost

Written by
Janet Bingham

Illustrated by
Rosalind Beardshaw

Silver and Sparkle were racing
through the woods.
"I'm winning!" called Silver.

Suddenly, he stopped.
Sparkle bumped into him —
thump!

"Look!" gasped Silver.
Shimmering white flakes were drifting down
from the sky. One landed on Sparkle's nose.
"It's cold!" she giggled in surprise.

Silver caught one on his tongue
and felt it melt. "It's wet, too," he said.
  "I think it's snow!" cried Sparkle,
dancing with excitement.
  "It's beautiful, just like Mommy said,
and it's…"
  "…fun!" added Silver. "Let's play!"

Soon the sky was full of snowflakes.
Silver chased them, and Sparkle
flicked them with her tail.
As the snow settled, Silver kicked
up little flurries, and Sparkle made
patterns with her footprints.

After a while the snowflakes stopped falling, and Silver and Sparkle gazed around. A blanket of snow lay over everything.

"I feel like I'm walking in the clouds!" laughed Sparkle.

The twins started to explore.
"Look, Sparkle," called Silver,
"berries!" He reached up to nibble
one, and nudged a branch. A dollop
of snow dropped onto his head!

"It looks like a hat," chuckled Sparkle.
Silver shook the snow off, sprinkling it everywhere.
"I can make it snow, too," he laughed.

Soon they came to a little clearing, at the
top of a gentle slope iced with snow.
   "Race you!" said Silver, as he set off down
the snowy hill. But his feet skidded and
slipped and —

Whoosh!

"Be careful!" cried Sparkle. But by the time Silver reached the bottom, he was laughing.

"That was a blast!" he said.
"I want to do it again!"

"Wait for me!" called Sparkle, and they slid down together, giggling all the way. It was so much fun, they did it again and again and again!

They didn't notice that more snow was falling as they played.

At last, they started to feel tired.
"I think it's time to go home," said Silver.

Sparkle looked around. "But which way is home?" she asked. "There's snow everywhere, and it all looks the same!"

"Don't be scared," said Silver bravely. "I think it's this way."
The little deer began to walk through the snow. It was very deep and it felt cold and heavy. They plodded on and on...

But after a while, they came back to the same spot.
"We're going around in circles!" cried Sparkle.
"We're lost!"

They looked around, wondering which way to go.
Then they heard a rustling in the trees. Someone
was coming towards them...

"Mommy!" the twins shouted happily. "We got lost!"

"You're safe now," said Mommy. "And we'll soon be home. What do you think of the snow?"

"We had fun," said Silver. "But it's cold and a bit hard to walk in," he added.

"You can follow in my footprints," said Mommy.
"It will be easier to walk that way."
So the twins set off, stepping safely in Mommy's tracks.

Suddenly, they saw a strange shape. Silver and
Sparkle jumped.

"Don't worry," laughed Mommy. "It's only a snowman.
I think someone made him just for us — look what's in
his basket."

"Carrots!" cried Silver, and they munched and
crunched until just one carrot was left. It was the
biggest carrot of all.

Silver reached up to take it, and — oops!
the snowman's hat slid onto Silver's head.
   "Now you've got a real hat!" Sparkle laughed.
Silver smiled proudly. And when they reached home,
he shared the last carrot with Sparkle.

At bedtime, Silver and Sparkle
snuggled up with Mommy.
"I love snow," murmured Sparkle sleepily.
"I love snow too," said Mommy. "Look
how it sparkles like silver in the moonlight!"

The twins stared at each other in surprise.
   "You gave us snow-names!" said Sparkle.
Mommy smiled and nodded,
   "That's because I love snow…" she said.

"... and I love **you**."